Copyright 2024 Ashley and Joshua Adventures

All rights reserved.

Printed in the United States

ISBN: 9798324207212

Meet the Black Crappie! Black crappies are a preferred species for many anglers due to their tendency to school and their delicious taste. They are found in quieter waters with plenty of vegetation.

Meet the Blue Jay! Blue jays are noisy, bold, and colorful birds with striking blue, white, and black plumage. They are very common in deciduous and coniferous forests and suburban areas.

Meet the Bluegill! Bluegills are part of the sunfish family and are known for their distinctive bright blue and orange colors and the dark spot at the rear of their gill cover.

**Meet the Bobcat! The bobcat is a sneaky, speedy kitty of the forest!
With its sharp eyes and quick paws, it hunts small animals like
rabbits and squirrels while creeping through the trees.**

Meet the Channel Catfish! They are common in Indiana's more significant streams and lakes. They have a slender, whiskered appearance and are bottom dwellers.

Meet the Cicadas! These insects are known for their loud, buzzing calls. Indiana periodically witnesses large emergences of 17-year cicadas, a significant event due to their mass numbers.

Meet the Common Snapping Turtle! Snapping turtles are giant and have powerful jaws. They prefer muddy water bodies where they can hide and ambush prey.

Meet the Coyote! The coyote is like a clever trickster of the wild! With its pointy ears and bushy tail, it roams the fields and forests, howling at the moon and hunting for tasty snacks like mice.

Meet the Eastern Box Turtle! This Turtle has a distinctive domed shell that can close completely to protect itself. It is commonly found in forested areas.

Meet the Eastern Carpenter Bee! Large and resembling bumblebees, carpenter bees are known for their ability to drill into wood to lay their eggs.

Meet the Eastern Chipmunk! The eastern chipmunk is a tiny bundle of energy in the woods! With its striped coat and cheeky grin, it scampers around, gathering nuts and seeds to stash away.

Meet the Eastern Cottontail! The eastern cottontail is a fluffy friend of the meadow! With its soft, cotton-like tail and big floppy ears, it hops around munching on tasty grass and clover.

Meet the Eastern Fence Lizard! These lizards are found in southern Indiana, especially in rocky and sunny habitats. They are known for their ability to change color slightly.

Meet the Eastern Gray Squirrel! The eastern gray squirrel is like a furry acrobat in the trees! With its bushy tail and nimble feet, it leaps from branch to branch, gathering nuts and seeds.

Meet the Eastern Mole! This tiny superhero of the underground world digs through the soil with its velvety fur and strong claws, creating intricate networks of tunnels.

Meet the Fireflies! Indiana is home to several species of fireflies, famous for their bright light emissions used during twilight to attract mates.

Meet the Great Horned Owl! Known for their tufted ears and intimidating yellow-eyed stare, great-horned owls are formidable nocturnal predators. They inhabit woods and forests across Indiana.

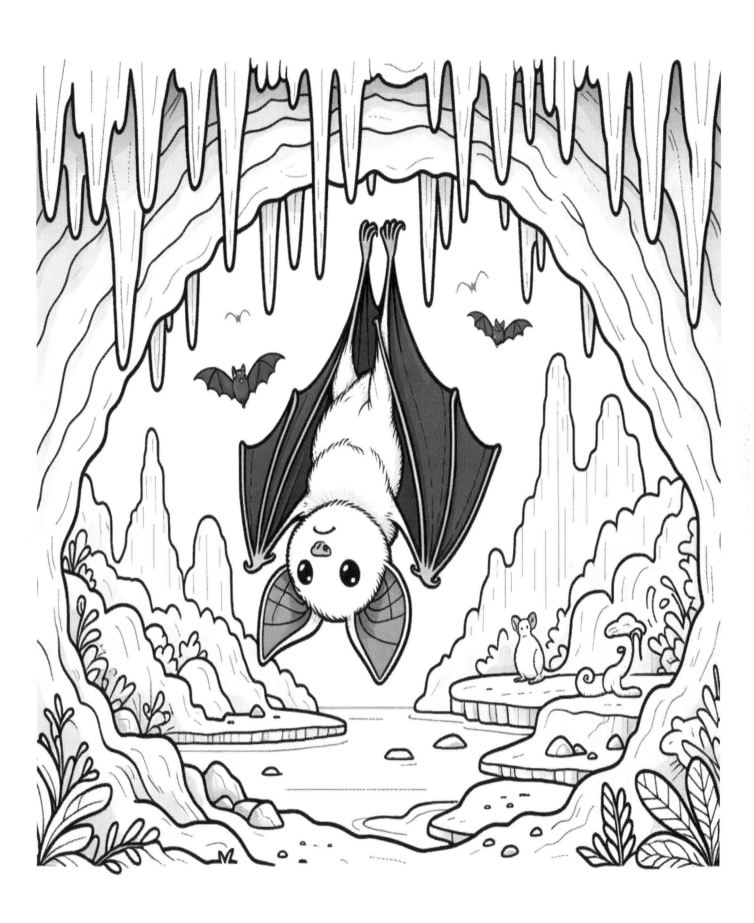

Meet the Indiana Bat! The Indiana bat is a tiny flyer of the night! With its dark fur and leathery wings, it flits through the air, gobbling up insects like mosquitoes and moths.

Meet the Indiana Dune Tiger Beetle! This critical species is found in Indiana Dunes National Park and has adapted to the dunes' sandy locations. It is known for its fast speed and striking coloration.

Meet the Indiana Warbler! This species, the "Yellow-throated Warbler," is often associated with Indiana due to its name. It is known for its bright yellow throat and is found in forests.

Meet the Ladybugs! Commonly seen in gardens, these beetles are valued for their appetite for aphids and other pests. The most common in Indiana is the seven-spotted ladybug.

Meet the Largemouth Bass! Largemouth bass are prevalent in lakes and slow-moving streams. They are recognized by their giant mouths that extend past their eyes and their robust body shape.

Meet the Little Brown Bat! The little brown bat is like a stealthy nighttime acrobat! With its dark fur and delicate wings, it swoops through the sky, gobbling up bugs like mosquitoes and beetles.

Meet the Luna Moth! The Luna moth is renowned for its beauty and has pale green wings and long, curving tail streamers. It is a nocturnal species, mostly seen at night.

Meet the Mink! The mink is like a sleek, speedy swimmer of the rivers and streams! With its shiny fur and webbed feet, it zips through the water, hunting for fish and frogs.

Meet the Monarch Butterfly! Perhaps the most recognizable of all North American butterflies, the monarch is known for its striking orange and black wings and remarkable migration from North America to central Mexico. Indiana is a waypoint in this migration.

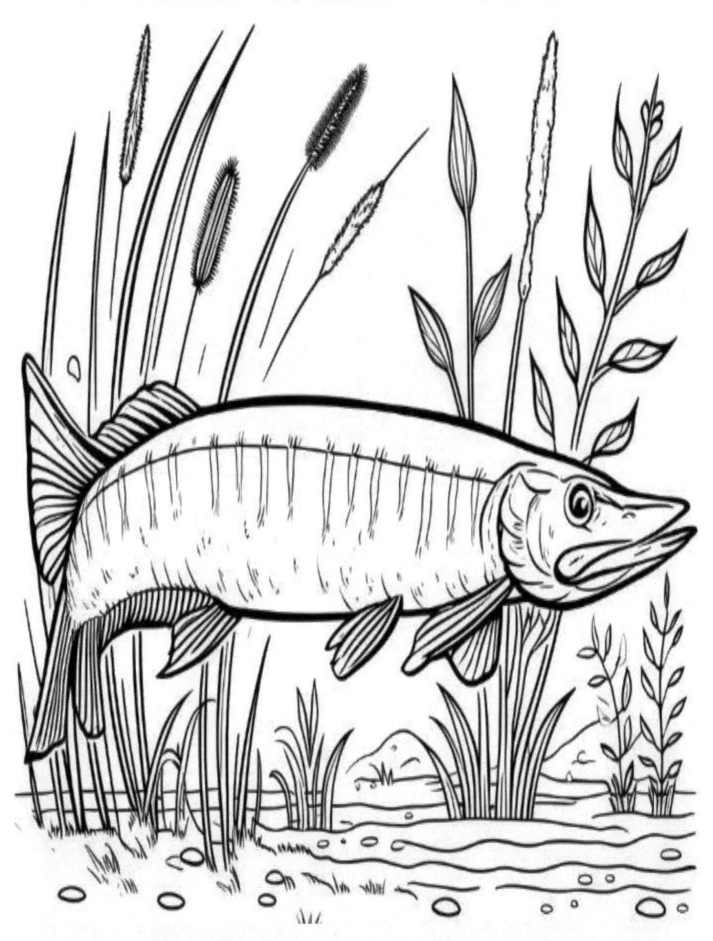

Meet the Muskellunge! Often called "muskie," these large, elusive fish are the largest of the pike family. They are prized by trophy anglers and are known for their size and decisive fight.

Meet the Muskrat! The muskrat is like a furry engineer of the wetlands! With its thick fur and paddle-like feet, it glides through the water, munching on plants and building cozy lodges.

Meet the Northern Cardinal! As the state bird of Indiana, the northern cardinal is popular and easily recognizable due to its bright red plumage in males and more subdued tones in females.

Meet the Northern Long-eared Bat! This shy, nighttime explorer of forests flutters through the darkness with its long ears and delicate wings, gobbling up insects.

Meet the northern pike! These aggressive fish have sharp teeth.
They are typically found in the more transparent waters of northern
Indiana, often lurking in weedy areas waiting for prey.

Meet the Opossum! This curious little marsupial explorer of the night wanders through the woods with its pointy nose and bushy tail, scavenging for tasty treats.

Meet the Pileated Woodpecker! The pileated woodpecker is easily recognized by its size, striking black and white markings, and the red crest on its head.

Meet the Praying Mantis! These predatory insects are known for their "praying" posture, with folded forearms. They are beneficial in gardens as they help control pest populations.

Meet the Raccoon! The raccoon is like a naughty masked bandit of the night! With its distinctive black "mask" and ringed tail, it rummages through garbage cans.

Meet the Red Fox! The red fox has a fluffy red coat and bushy tail; it dashes through the forest, hunting for mice and rabbits while sometimes playing chase games with its fox friends.

Meet the Red-tailed Hawk! The red-tailed hawk often perches along roadways or soaring high in the sky. They are identified by their broad, rounded wings and a characteristic red tail.

Meet the River Otter! The river otter is like a playful swimmer of the streams! With its sleek, waterproof fur and webbed feet, it dives and frolics through the water, chasing after fish and crayfish.

Meet the Sandhill Crane! These tall, stately birds are best known for their large size and distinctive red forehead. They migrate through Indiana, particularly at the Jasper-Pulaski Fish and Wildlife Area.

Meet the Sauger! Similar to walleye but generally smaller, sauger thrive in cloudy river environments. They are well-adapted to low-light conditions and are found in the Ohio River and its streams.

Meet the Smallmouth Bass! The smallmouth bass inhabit calmer and clearer water than their largemouth cousins. They are typically found in rocky areas of rivers and lakes.

Meet the Spotted Lanternfly! Though not native and considered invasive, the spotted lanternfly has been found in Indiana. Due to its wide range of host plants, it poses a threat to various crops.

Meet the Spotted Turtle! This small turtle is easily recognized by the yellow spots on its dark shell. They prefer wetland habitats but are increasingly rare due to habitat loss and collection for the pet trade.

Meet the Striped Skunk! With its unique stripes and bushy tail, it shuffles through fields and forests, sniffing out tasty insects and plants while using its special spray to defend itself from predators.

Meet the Walleye! They are found in lakes and rivers of Indiana. They have a distinctive olive and gold coloring, and their eyes reflect light, aiding their vision in low light, a distinctive trait.

Meet the White-tailed Deer! With its big brown eyes and fluffy white tail, it prances through the trees, nibbling on leaves and grass while watching for any signs of danger.

**Meet the Wood Duck! Wood ducks are stunningly colorful ducks.
They breed in wooded swamps and marshes across Indiana, using
tree holes and artificial nest boxes as nesting sites.**

Meet the Woodchuck! The woodchuck is like a chunky digger of the fields! With its sturdy body and short legs, it burrows into the ground, munching on plants and vegetables.

Meet the Yellow Perch! Yellow perch are a popular species among Indiana ice fishermen. They have distinctive vertical stripes in many of the state's lakes.

Made in the USA
Columbia, SC
10 May 2024